A Gift For:

Addison

From:

Ga Ga

Copyright © 2011 Hallmark Licensing, Inc.

Published by Hallmark Gift Books,
a division of Hallmark Cards, Inc.,
Kansas City, MO 64141
Visit us on the Web at www.Hallmark.com.

Editor: Lindsay Evans
Art Director: Kevin Swanson
Designer: Scott Swanson
Production Artist: Bryan Ring

ISBN: 978-1-59530-364-6
BOK1175

Printed and bound in China
NOV11

Hallmark
GIFT BOOKS

BiG SiSTERS ARE Sweet

By Tom Shay-Zapien
Illustrated by Maria Sarria

The day a family welcomes home a new baby, a big sister is born.

A big sister doesn't always realize it, but she's just about the best gift a little brother or little sister could ever get.

Being older means she's seen oodles
and learned heaps...

...which means she has plenty to show and tell her new little friend.

Becoming a big sister is extra special for all kinds of reasons.

Being **big** makes her hands extra helpful.

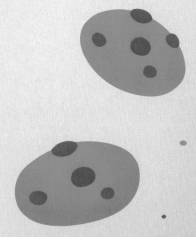

Being **big** makes her heart extra brave.

Being **big** makes her funny bone extra silly.

Being **big** makes her inside voice extra soft. (Sometimes.)

Being **big** makes her tricks extra amazing.

Being **big** makes her moods extra patient.

Being **big** makes her ideas extra fun.

Being **big** makes her laughter extra sweet.

Being **big** makes her stories extra exciting.

Being **big** makes looking up to her extra easy.

But best of all, being such a great big sister always makes her extra loved.

If you have enjoyed this book
and are proud of your big-sister status,
we would love to hear from you.

Please send your comments to:
Hallmark Book Feedback
P.O. Box 419034
Mail Drop 215
Kansas City, MO 64141

Or e-mail us at:
booknotes@hallmark.com